A Note to Parents and Caregivers:

Read-it! Readers are for children who are just starting on the amazing road to reading. These beautiful books support both the acquisition of reading skills and the love of books. In some books, there are common sounds at the beginning, the ending, or even in the middle of many familiar words. It is good preparation for reading to help students listen for and repeat these sounds as part of having fun with words.

The RED LEVEL presents familiar topics using common words and repeating sentence patterns.

The BLUE LEVEL presents new ideas using a larger vocabulary and varied sentence structure.

The YELLOW LEVEL presents more challenging ideas, a broad vocabulary, and wide variety in sentence structure.

The GREEN LEVEL presents more complex ideas, an extended vocabulary range, and expanded language structures.

When sharing a book with your child, read in short stretches, pausing often to talk about the pictures. Have your child turn the pages and point to the pictures and familiar words. And be sure to reread favorite stories or parts of stories.

There is no right or wrong way to share books with children. Find time to read with your child, and pass on the legacy of literacy.

Adria F. Klein, Ph.D.
Professor Emeritus
California State University
San Bernardino, California

Managing Editors: Bob Temple, Catherine Neitge
Creative Director: Terri Foley
Editors: Jerry Ruff, Patricia Stockland
Editorial Adviser: Mary Lindeen
Designer: Amy Bailey Muehlenhardt
Storyboard development: Charlene DeLage
Page production: Picture Window Books
The illustrations in this book were prepared digitally.

Picture Window Books
5115 Excelsior Boulevard
Suite 232
Minneapolis, MN 55416
877-845-8392
www.picturewindowbooks.com

Printed in the United States of America.

Library of Congress Cataloging-in-Publication Data
Blackaby, Susan.
Sunny bumps the drum / by Susan Blackaby ; illustrated by Amy Bailey Muehlenhardt.
p. cm. — (Read-it! readers classroom tales)
Summary: Sunny and the others prepare to perform in the school Spring Sing.
ISBN 1-4048-0587-7 (hardcover)
[1. Singing—Fiction. 2. Concerts—Fiction. 3. Schools—Fiction.]
I. Muehlenhardt, Amy Bailey, 1974- ill. II. Title. III. Series.
PZ7.B5318Su 2004
[E]—dc22 2004007391

Sunny Bumps the Drum

By Susan Blackaby

Illustrated by Amy Bailey Muehlenhardt

Special thanks to our advisers for their expertise:
Adria F. Klein, Ph.D.
Professor Emeritus, California State University
San Bernardino, California

Susan Kesselring, M.A.
Literacy Educator
Rosemount-Apple Valley-Eagan (Minnesota) School District

PICTURE WINDOW BOOKS
Minneapolis, Minnesota

“Here we are for music class,” said Mrs. Shay. “Mr. Hunt will get you set for the Spring Sing.”

The Spring Sing was big stuff. All the moms and dads came to hear the kids.

"Hello," said Mr. Hunt. "We will sing 'You Are My Sunshine.' Maybe some of you know it."

Mr. Hunt hummed the song.

Sunny hummed it, too.

“My dad sings that all the time,” said Sunny. “It is his favorite song.”

"Good!" said Mr. Hunt. "You can help us learn the song."

Mr. Hunt was funny. He had fuzzy eyebrows. They hopped and jumped in time to the music.

"Watch my cuffs," he said. He held up his arms to lead the kids.

The kids worked hard to get set for the Spring Sing. They sang the song a bunch of times.

“Let’s run through it once more!” said Mr. Hunt.

They went up and down from the stage a hundred times.

"No clunking up the stairs,"
said Mr. Hunt.

"On the day of the Spring Sing, you will be all set," said Mr. Hunt. "You sound great."

The day of the Spring Sing came.
The kids were a bundle of nerves.

Spring Sing Today

"I have butterflies in my tummy," said Sunny.

"So do I," said Bob.

“Me too,” said Vic.

Jess and Kat nodded.

The kids shuffled to the stage.

Mr. Hunt held up his arms.

He raised his eyebrows.

The kids started to sing.

Jess came in too soon. Kat came in too late. Vic sang too loud.

Sunny held the note too long.

Bob jumbled the words.

It sounded awful.

Mr. Hunt waved his arms like mad. His eyebrows wiggled like caterpillars.

Sunny's legs were shaking. Her knees buckled. BUMP! THUMP! BOOM!

Sunny tipped over. She tumbled into the drum. The kids stopped singing.

Bob gave Sunny a tug to help her up. She dusted herself off.

“Clumsy me,” Sunny mumbled.

Then Vic chuckled. So did Mr. Hunt. So did Sunny. So did everyone else.

"Let's take it from the top," said Mr. Hunt. Up went his arms. Up went his eyebrows.

This time the kids did not miss a beat. They sounded great.

They were almost done with the song. They had one note to go. Sunny's dad jumped up.

He clapped too soon. He clapped too long. He clapped too loud. It sounded great.

Levels for *Read-it!* Readers

Read-it! Readers help children practice early reading skills with brightly illustrated stories.

Red Level: Familiar topics with frequently used words and repeating patterns.

I Am in Charge of Me by Dana Meachen Rau
Let's Share by Dana Meachen Rau

Blue Level: New ideas with a larger vocabulary and a variety of language structures.

At the Beach by Patricia M. Stockland
The Playground Snake by Brian Moses
The Word of the Day by Susan Blackaby

Yellow Level: Challenging ideas with an expanded vocabulary and a wide variety of sentences.

A Fire Drill with Mr. Dill by Susan Blackaby
Hatching Chicks by Susan Blackaby
Marvin, The Blue Pig by Karen Wallace
Moo! by Penny Dolan
Pippin's Big Jump by Hilary Robinson
A Pup Shows Up by Susan Blackaby
The Queen's Dragon by Anne Cassidy
Tired of Waiting by Dana Meachen Rau

Green Level: More complex ideas with an extended vocabulary range and expanded language structures.

Classroom Cookout by Susan Blackaby
Clever Cat by Karen Wallace
Flora McQuack by Penny Dolan
Izzie's Idea by Jillian Powell
Naughty Nancy by Anne Cassidy
The Roly-Poly Rice Ball by Penny Dolan
Sausages! by Anne Adeney
Sunny Bumps the Drum by Susan Blackaby
The Truth About Hansel and Gretel by Karina Law

A complete list of _Read-it!_ Readers is available on our Web site: www.picturewindowbooks.com